W9-CNQ-766

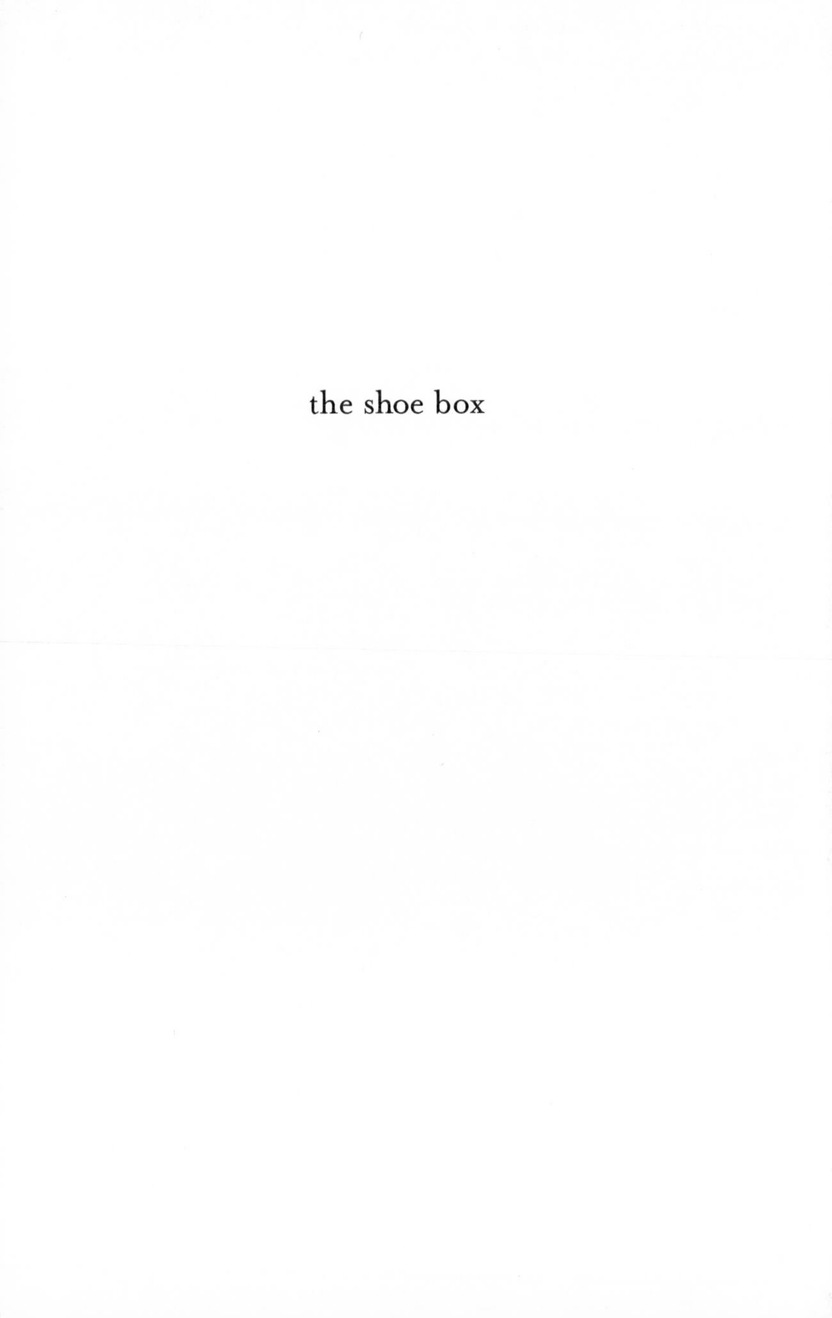

the shoe box

THE SHOE BOX

A CHRISTMAS STORY BY

FRANCINE RIVERS

TYNDALE HOUSE PUBLISHERS, INC.
WHEATON, ILLINOIS

Visit Tyndale's exciting Web site at www.tyndale.com

Designed by Jackie Noe

"The Shoe Box" was originally published in the anthology *Christmas by the Hearth,* copyright © 1996 by Tyndale House Publishers, Inc., Wheaton, Illinois.

Scripture quotations are taken from the *Holy Bible,* New Living Translation, copyright © 1996. Used by permission of Tyndale House Publishers, Inc., Wheaton, Illinois 60189. All rights reserved.

Library of Congress Cataloging-in-Publication Data

Rivers, Francine, date
The shoe box / Francine Rivers.
p. cm.
"The shoe box" was originally published in the anthology "Christmas by the Hearth," copyright © 1996 by Tyndale House Publishers.
ISBN 0-8423-1901-8
I. Christmas by the hearth. II Title.
PS3568.I83165S46 1999
813'.54—dc21 99-34161

Printed in the United States of America

05 04 03 02 01 00 99
9 8 7 6 5 4 3 2

Contents

How This Story Came to Be

When I first became a Christian, one of the hardest things for me to do was give my burdens to the Lord. I would worry over all kinds of things. I remember a friend talking about putting prayers in a lunch bag, and that got me thinking. One of the many jobs I had held was that of a secretary, and I remembered the "in" and "out" boxes. From that memory came the idea of a "God box." I took an ordinary cardboard container with a lid and covered it with beautiful wrapping paper. Then I cut a slot in the top. Whenever something was bothering me greatly and I couldn't let it go, I would write out a prayer about it. Then I would tuck the written prayer into the God box. Sometimes my husband and my children would write prayers and tuck them into the box as well. It was amazing to me how this physical exercise helped me give up worries and burdens to the Lord. Every few months I would open the box and read the prayers. What I found was a source of great joy and comfort, for many of the prayers were answered, often in completely unexpected ways.

My God box gave me the idea for "The Shoe Box." While I put worries and burdens in my box, I wanted Timmy to put blessings and praises in his box as well. It reminded me that there are all kinds of prayers—worship and praise as well as cries for help. Scripture says the prayers of believers are the sweet scent of incense to the Lord.

RUNNING SHOES
RUNNING SHOES

Timmy O'Neil came to live with Mary and David Holmes on a cloudy day in the middle of September, two weeks after school started. He was a quiet little six-year-old boy with sorrowful eyes. Not very long afterward, they wondered about the box he carried with him all the time. It was an ordinary shoe box with a red lid and the words *Running Shoes* printed on one side.

Timmy carried it everywhere he went. When he put it down, it was always where he could see it.

"Should we ask him about it?" Mary said to her husband.

"No. He'll talk to us about it when he's ready," David said, but he was as curious as she was.

Even Mrs. Iverson, the social worker, was curious about the shoe box. She told Mary and David that

Timmy had the box when the policeman brought him to the Youth Authority offices. Timmy's dad was put in prison. His mom had a job, but she didn't make enough to take proper care of Timmy. A lady in the apartment house where he lived found out he was by himself all day and reported it to the police.

"They brought him to me with one small suitcase of clothes and that shoe box," Mrs. Iverson said. "I asked him what was inside it, and he said, 'Things.' But what things he wouldn't tell me."

Even the children at Timmy's new school were curious about the box. He didn't put it in his cubbyhole like things the other children brought. He would put it on top of his desk while he did his work.

His first grade teacher, Mrs. King,

was curious, too. "What do you have there, Timmy?"

"My box," he said.

"What's in your box?"

"Things," he said and went on with his arithmetic.

Mrs. King didn't ask him about the box again. She liked Timmy, and she didn't want to pry. She told Mary and David that Timmy was a good student. He wasn't the brightest by far, but he always did his best work. Mrs. King admired that about Timmy. She wrote a note to him about it on one of his math papers. "Other students will learn by your example," the note said, and she drew a big smiling face on his paper and gave him a pretty, sparkly star sticker.

Mary Holmes learned that Timmy liked chocolate chip cookies, so she kept the cookie jar full. Timmy would come home from school on the yellow bus and sit at the kitchen table, the box under his chair. Mary always sat with him and asked him about his day while he had milk and cookies.

Timmy asked Mary one day why she and David didn't have any children of their own. Mary said she had asked God the same question over and over.

She said while she waited for an answer, she was thankful to have him.

Every evening when he came home from work, David played catch with Timmy in the backyard. Timmy always brought the box outside with him and set it on the lawn chair where he could see it.

Timmy even took the shoe box with him to Sunday school. He sat between Mary and David, the box in his lap.

When he went to bed at night, the

shoe box sat on the nightstand beside his bed.

Timmy got letters from his mother twice a week. Once she sent him ten dollars and a short note from his father. Timmy cried when Mary read it to him because his father said how much he missed Timmy and how sorry he was that he had made such a big mistake. Mary held Timmy on her lap in the rocking chair for a long time.

Chocolate Chip Cookies

One of my fondest memories is of my mother making chocolate chip cookies. All through my childhood, she would keep the cookie jar full of them. When I grew up and had children of my own, Mom would bake chocolate chip cookies just before I would bring our children up to Oregon for a summer visit. The first thing I would do after greeting my mother and father was head for that cookie jar! Yum!! And my children were right on my heels.

After my mother and father both passed away, I started baking chocolate chip cookies for our home Bible study class. Every Tuesday afternoon, I'm in the kitchen, baking. And every time I do, I *think of my mother. There is nothing like the smell of freshly baked chocolate chip cookies to stir sweet memories.*

- 1 cup (2 sticks) butter, softened
- ¾ cup granulated sugar
- ¾ cup packed brown sugar
- 2 eggs
- 2 tsp. vanilla extract
- 1 tsp. baking soda
- 1 tsp. salt
- 2¼ cups all-purpose flour
- 1 cup semisweet chocolate chips
- ½ cup white chocolate chips

Combine butter, sugars, eggs, and vanilla extract in large bowl. Stir until creamy. Mix baking soda and salt with flour and add to the large bowl. Stir everything together, and add the dark and white chocolate chips. (You can add nuts as well. Chopped pecans, macadamia nuts, or walnuts are best. I've also added raisins.)

Drop by spoonfuls onto baking sheet. Bake at 350 degrees until golden brown.

When David came home, they took Timmy out for a pizza dinner and then to the theater to see an animated movie about a lion. Mary and David both noticed Timmy's expression of wonder and delight.

When Timmy got off the school bus the next day, he was surprised to find David waiting for him. "Hi, Champ," David said. "I thought I'd come home early and share your special day." He ruffled Timmy's hair and walked with him to the house.

When they came in the kitchen door, Mary leaned down and kissed Timmy on the cheek. "Happy birthday, Timmy."

His eyes widened in surprise as he saw a big box wrapped with pretty paper and tied up with bright-colored ribbons on the kitchen table.

"It's for you, Timmy," David said. "You can open it."

Timmy put his old shoe box carefully on the table and then opened the bigger box with the pretty paper. In it he found a lion just like the one in the movie. Hugging it, he laughed.

Mary turned away quickly and fussed with the candles on the birthday cake so Timmy wouldn't see the tears in her eyes. David noticed and smiled at her. It was the first time she and David had seen Timmy smile or laugh about anything. And it made them very happy.

When Mary put the birthday cake on the table and lit the candles, David took her hand and then Timmy's and said a prayer of blessing and thanksgiving. "Go ahead, Timmy. Make a wish and blow out the candles." Timmy didn't have to think very long about what he wished, and when he blew, not a candle was left burning.

Timmy's mother came to visit every other week. She and Timmy sat together in the living room. She asked him questions about school and the Holmeses and if he was happy with them. He said he was, but he still missed her. She held him and stroked his hair back from his face and kissed him. She told him she missed him, too, but it was more important that he have a safe place to grow up. "These are nice people, Timmy. You won't grow up like I did."

Each time before she left, she always told him to be good and remember what she'd taught him. She picked him up and held him tightly for a long time before she kissed him and put him down again. Timmy was always sad and quiet when she left.

RUNNING SHOES

Fall came, and the leaves on the maple tree in the backyard turned brilliant gold. Sometimes Timmy would go outside and sit with his back against the trunk of the tree, his shoe box in his lap, and just watch the leaves flutter in the cool breeze.

Mary's mother and father came for Thanksgiving. Mary had gotten up very early in the morning and started preparing pies while David stuffed the turkey. Timmy liked Mary's mother and father. Mary's mother played Monopoly with him, and her father told him funny and exciting fishing stories.

Friends came to join them for Thanksgiving dinner, and the house was full of happy people. Timmy had never seen so much food on one table before. He tried everything. When dinner was over, David gave him the wishbone. He told Timmy to let it dry and then they'd pull on it to see who would get their wish.

A Fishing Story

When we visited Hawaii years ago when the children were small, we stayed at the Coco Palms Resort on the island of Kauai. They had a lagoon filled with beautiful carp. They supplied the children with fishing rods and bread. The hooks were not barbed, so the children could catch fish and release them. They had hours of fun this way, and no harm came to the fish, who were always hungry!

Lil Ogden's Pie Crust

There is a lady in our church who is famous for her fantastic pies. Every year, we have a pie auction in which the youth raise money for a missions project. Lil Ogden's pies have gone for as much as seventy-five dollars. She has a servant's heart and is dedicated to prayer. And she's also a great cook!

Utensils

Large bowl

Rolling pin

Pastry blender

Measuring spoons

Flour sifter

Measuring cup

Spatula or kitchen knife

Pastry brush

Breadboard

Ingredients

1 tsp. salt

3 cups flour

1 ½ cups vegetable shortening

1 egg

1 tbsp. vinegar

5 tbsp. cold water

Mix salt and flour. Cut in shortening until fine. Mix egg, vinegar, and water together and beat with fork. Add liquid to flour mixture and stir well. Place half the dough on a floured breadboard; dust with flour and work enough into the dough to keep it from sticking. Roll out to fit size of pie plate.

Francine's Apple Pie Filling

The best apples for a pie are Gravenstein. They're available in late summer. We buy them by the lug at the orchard here in Sonoma County.

6–8 apples (peeled and sliced)
1 tbsp. butter
1 tsp. cinnamon
Dash of nutmeg
¾ cup sugar
1 tbsp. flour

RUNNING SHOES

December came and brought with it colder weather. Mary and David bought Timmy a heavy snow parka and gloves. His mother gave him a new backpack, and he put his shoe box in it. He carried it to school each day, and in the afternoon he'd hang the backpack on the closet door, where he could see it while he was doing his homework or when he went to bed at night.

It seemed everybody in the small town where Mary and David Holmes and Timmy lived knew about the shoe box. But nobody but Timmy knew what was inside it.

A few boys tried to take it from him one day, but Mrs. King saw them and made them pick up trash on the school grounds during lunch hour.

Sometimes children on the bus

would ask him what he had in the box, but he'd say, "Just things."

"What kind of things?"

He would shrug, but he would never say.

Turkey Dressing

This turkey dressing recipe was passed down from Grandma Johnson to my father-in-law, Bill Rivers. Dad Bill knew just how to cook a turkey. I never tasted one that wasn't perfect. It's been a family tradition, ever since he learned from Grandma, for each generation of men to teach the next. Dad Bill taught Rick, and Rick has taught Trevor, our eldest son. Rick also flew back East to teach our daughter, Shannon, and her husband,

Rich, how to roast a Thanksgiving turkey à la Rivers. Travis, our youngest son, will be the next to learn, when he has a family of his own.

2 LARGE (OR 3 SMALL) ONIONS
7 STALKS OF CELERY
1 LARGE GREEN BELL PEPPER
2 (OR 3) 6-OZ. PACKAGES OF CROUTONS
TURKEY GIBLETS
ENOUGH TURKEY BROTH TO DAMPEN STUFFING

GRIND EVERYTHING AND MIX TOGETHER. WASH INSIDE AND OUTSIDE OF TURKEY CAREFULLY. OIL INSIDE AND OUTSIDE OF TURKEY; SALT INSIDE AND OUTSIDE OF TURKEY (LIBERALLY). STUFF THE BIRD WITH YUMMY DRESSING.

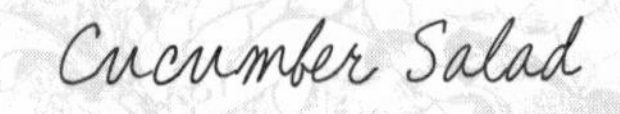

Cucumber Salad

This is another favorite from Grandma Johnson.

- 1 LARGE CUCUMBER, THINLY SLICED
- 1 CUP WHITE VINEGAR
- ½ CUP SUGAR
- ½ TSP. SALT
- 2 TBSP. CHOPPED PARSLEY
- DASH OF PEPPER
- ½ TSP. DILL WEED

PRESS CUCUMBER SLICES BETWEEN PAPER TOWELS TO DRY. MIX REMAINING INGREDIENTS TOGETHER. ADD CUCUMBERS. REFRIGERATE FOR 3 HOURS.

Grandma Johnson's Swedish Meatballs

6 zwieback
2 eggs
8 oz. sour cream
2 or 3 onions, chopped
butter
3 lbs. ground round
3 lbs. ground lean pork (boneless pork chops)
1 tbsp. sugar
1 tbsp. salt
1 tbsp. allspice
½ tsp. pepper
¾ cup mashed potatoes

Soak zwieback in eggs and sour cream until softened; crush and mix well. Brown onions in a small amount of butter. Mix meats and spices together in large bowl. Add onions, zwieback mixture, and mashed potatoes. Mix well.

Roll mixture into balls the size of a walnut. Brown in a large skillet. Sprinkle more allspice on meat as it's cooking. Cover with water and cook over low heat for 15 minutes. Do not boil.

Grandma Johnson's Swedish Korv

First, prepare sausage casings (use medium size in 36-inch lengths). Soak for one hour to defrost; wash off salt by attaching end to faucet and slowly filling with water. Run water very slowly. Check for holes in casings.

Mix together (like a meatloaf):

- 3 lbs. lean ground beef
- 3 lbs. pork butt, coarse ground
- 3 lbs. potatoes, ground
- 3 medium yellow onions, ground
- 2 tbsp. salt
- ¾ tsp. allspice
- ½ tsp. pepper
- 1 can consommé

Add a little water if too dry. Should be the consistency of turkey dressing.

Cut up 8 stalks of celery, and add to a large soup pot full of water. Bring to a boil.

Put casings on food grinder. (Putting the casings on the grinder is like putting on nylons. Be careful not to make holes!) Leave 4 inches dangling.

One person feeds meat/potato/spice mixture into the machine while another person holds the filling casing. Leave 3–4 inches on each end for expansion while cooking. Gently work out any bubbles or prick carefully with a pin. Rinse in sink full of warm water. Check for air bubbles.

Cook korv sections in boiling celery water 20–25 minutes (until whitish) for freezing; cook 40 minutes if serving right away. Freeze in large round containers with broth. Take out of freezer a day ahead. Cook for 20 minutes.

Serve hot with sweet mustard. Recipe makes 12–14 feet of sausage. Korv broth makes great soup stock.

The church where Mary and David Holmes took Timmy had a Christmas program each year. The choir practiced for two months to present the community with a cantata. Everyone dressed in costumes. This year part of the program was to include acting out the Nativity while the choir sang.

"We need lots of children to volunteer for the parts," Chuck, the program director, said. "The choir will sing about the angels who came to speak to the shepherds in the fields. And there's a song about the wise men who came from faraway lands to see Jesus. And, of course, we need a girl to play Mary and a boy to play Joseph."

"What about Jesus?" Timmy said.

"Latasha has a baby brother," one of the girls said. "Why don't you let her be Mary, and her baby brother can be Jesus?"

"That's a great idea," Chuck said.

Most of the children were eager to be part of the play. Even Timmy, but he was too shy to raise his hand. Chuck noticed the look on his face when all the parts were filled. He asked his helper to get the children started in a game and took Timmy aside. "We could use another shepherd in the play," he said carefully. "Would you like to be a shepherd?"

"I'd like to be a wise man."

There were already three wise men, but Chuck thought about it and nodded his head. "You know, the Bible doesn't say how many wise men came to see Jesus. There might have been four. There might have been more than that. I'll talk to the lady making costumes and ask her if she can make one more for you."

The lady was very pleased to make

a costume for Timmy. She spent extra time on it because she wanted it to be very special. She made a long blue tunic that went to his ankles. She made a wide multicolored sash and an outer garment like an open robe of a beautiful brocade with purple and gold. Then she made a turban and put a big rhinestone brooch on the front and some colored plumes in the top.

Friends gave us a beautiful Nativity scene for Christmas the year Rick and I became Christians. The set of figurines is made of blue-and-white porcelain. It's always the first thing I put out when I begin decorating for Christmas shortly after Thanksgiving. Over the past few years, Rick and I have purchased several other Nativity sets. We have a large one on display in the living room, the blue-and-white one in the dining room, and another smaller set in our upstairs bedroom.

Nativity sets make wonderful gifts. When we were in the Holy Land a few years ago, we purchased a hand-carved olive-wood Nativity set in Bethlehem for our daughter, Shannon, and her husband, Rich. Our elder son, Trevor, married Jenny, and we have started a Nativity set for them as well. Theirs is hand painted and comes from Rome. We will be adding pieces year by year. I hope one day to have Nativity sets in every room, perhaps even one large enough to put on our roof! That way, people will see it from the freeway and be reminded that we are celebrating Jesus' birth. May none of us ever forget that Jesus is the reason for the season and the greatest gift of all!

RUNNING SHOES

When the night came for the program, everyone was so excited that no one noticed that Timmy was still holding his old shoe box instead of the fancy wooden jewelry box he was supposed to carry onto the stage. Everyone did notice when he followed the other three wise men out of the wings and into the lights.

One by one the wise men approached the manger and left their gifts, but everyone sitting in the audience in the big church social hall was looking at Timmy. Timmy's mother had come to see him in the cantata. Mrs. Iverson, the social worker, had come as well. So had Mrs. King and two other teachers from Timmy's school.

They were all holding their breath when it came Timmy's turn to put his kingly offering before the manger, where the baby Jesus was sleeping. He looked like a small regal king in his royal garb, the turban and jewel on his head. The lights were on him, and the sparkles in the pretty clothes made him shine. He carried the old, worn shoe box with the red lid and the words *Running Shoes* in both hands and presented it with solemn respect to the child in the manger.

Then Timmy straightened and turned and smiled broadly at his mother, Mary and David, Mrs. Iverson, and Mrs. King and her two friends before he took his place among the other wise men at the far side of the stage.

They all let out their breath in relief, but they also sat wondering and watching Timmy. He was singing with the choir, not the least bit concerned about the precious shoe box he had left on the far side of the stage. In fact, he didn't look at it once. And they'd never seen him look so happy.

My favorite Christmas music is Handel's Messiah. The music was composed in 1741 in twenty-four days, from August 22 to September 14. That such a beautiful work of music was written in so short a time is nothing short of miraculous! Messiah was first performed for charitable purposes in Dublin, Ireland, on April 13, 1742. Handel himself conducted. Ever since this work was heard, it has been a favorite. Every year, here in Sonoma County, California, there is a "Sing-Along Messiah" at the Luther Burbank Center for the Arts. Friends invited me four years ago, and even though I can barely carry a tune, I went. I have been been going ever since. It is glorious to sing with a multitude. Many who come to the performance are not Christians, but they are hearing and proclaiming the Word of God through this inspired music. I always come away feeling joyful over the birth of our Savior, Jesus Christ, the Lord.

When the cantata was over, his mother took his hand and went with him for Christmas punch and cookies. Mary and David went with them. So did Mrs. Iverson and Mrs. King and the two teachers who had come with her. They all said how proud they were of him and what a good job he did.

When it came time to go, Timmy's mother asked him if he wanted to go and get his shoe box.

"Oh no," Timmy said. "I gave it to Jesus."

They all were curious about what was inside the shoe box, but when they passed by the stage, they saw it was gone. Timmy noticed, too, but he didn't seem the least bit upset about it. In fact, he smiled.

The hymn Timmy and his friends sang in the cantata

What Child is this, who, laid to rest, on Mary's lap is sleeping?

Whom angels greet with anthems sweet, while shepherds watch are keeping?

This, this is Christ the King, whom shepherds guard and angels sing;

Haste, haste to bring Him laud, the babe, the son of Mary.

Why lies He in such mean estate where ox and ass are feeding?

Good Christian; fear, for sinners here the silent Word is pleading.

This, this is Christ the King, whom shepherds guard and angels sing;

Haste, haste to bring Him laud, the babe, the son of Mary.

So bring Him incense, gold, and myrrh, come, peasant, king, to own Him;

The King of kings salvation brings, let loving hearts enthrone Him.

This, this is Christ the King, whom shepherds guard and angels sing;

Haste, haste to bring Him laud, the babe, the son of Mary.

—William C. Dix

UNNING SHOES
Dear Timmy,
I really miss you so
much. I'm sorry I made
such a big mistake
and be away
you for
while
ADMIT ONE

Here it is, my Lord," the angel said, kneeling before the throne of God. He held the old, worn shoe box with the words *Running Shoes* printed on it and set it at God's feet.

Jesus took it and set it upon his lap. He put his hand over it and looked out at the gathering of thousands of angels and seraphim and saints. Even they were curious about what was inside. Only he and Timmy knew.

Peter the apostle was there and, bold as always, was the only one who dared ask, "What's in that box, Lord? What has the child given you?"

"Just things," Jesus said, smiling. He had watched Timmy from the time he was conceived. He had counted every hair upon his head and knew all that was in his heart. And he had waited for the day when the child would come to him with what he had to offer.

Jesus took the top off the shoe box, and all the angels and seraphim and saints leaned forward as he took out one item at a time and laid it tenderly upon his lap.

And what they saw were *just things*—very simple, very ordinary things:

The worn and faded silk edge of his
baby blanket
A wedding picture of his mother and
father

His mother's letters with a rubber
band around them
Ten dollars
His father's note of love and apology
A math paper with a smiley face and a
note from his teacher
A pretty star sticker
A movie ticket stub
Used birthday candles with dried
icing on them wrapped in pretty

wrapping paper and tied with a
bright curled ribbon

The big side of a broken turkey wishbone

A pretty red maple leaf

An old baseball

And six chocolate chip cookies

There were unseen things, too. Hopes, dreams, prayers, and many worries and fears. All of them were in the box Timmy gave to the Lord.

Jesus put everything back in the shoe box with tender care. He put the red lid back on the box and then rested his hands upon it as he looked at the multitude before him. "Timmy has given the most precious gift of all: the faith of a child."

More angels were sent to guard Timmy from that day forth. They never left his side.

They were with Timmy when Mary

and David invited his mother to come and live with them. She had a room right across the hall from Timmy. The angels were with him when Mary and David had a baby of their own. They were with him when his father got out of prison in time for his high school graduation. They surrounded Timmy as he grew up, married, and had children of his own.

In fact, angels surrounded him and

protected him all the days of his life up until the very moment he was ushered into heaven, straight into the waiting arms of the Lord who loved him.

The Christmas Story

SELECTED FROM MATTHEW 1–2 AND LUKE 1–2

NEW LIVING TRANSLATION

Now this is how Jesus the Messiah was born. God sent the angel Gabriel to Nazareth, a village in Galilee, to a virgin named Mary. She was engaged to be married to a man named Joseph, a descendant of King David. Gabriel appeared to her and said, "Greetings, favored woman! The Lord is with you!"

Confused and disturbed, Mary tried to think what the angel could mean. "Don't be frightened, Mary," the angel told her, "for God has decided to bless you! You will become pregnant and have a son, and you are to name him Jesus. He will be very great and will be called the Son of the Most High. And the Lord God will give him the throne of his ancestor David. And he will reign over Israel forever; his Kingdom will never end!"

Mary asked the angel, "But how can I have a baby? I am a virgin."

The angel replied, "The Holy Spirit will come upon you, and the power of the Most High will overshadow you. So the baby born to you will be holy, and he will be called the

Son of God. What's more, your relative Elizabeth has become pregnant in her old age! People used to say she was barren, but she's already in her sixth month. For nothing is impossible with God."

Mary responded, "I am the Lord's servant, and I am willing to accept whatever he wants. May everything you have said come true." And then the angel left.

While she was still a virgin, she became pregnant by the Holy Spirit. Joseph, her fiancé, being a just man, decided to break the engagement quietly, so as not to disgrace her publicly.

As he considered this, he fell asleep, and an angel of the Lord appeared to him in a dream. "Joseph, son of David," the angel said, "do not be afraid to go ahead with your marriage to Mary. For the child within her has been conceived by the Holy Spirit. And she will have a son, and you are to name him Jesus, for he will save his people from their sins." All of this happened to fulfill the Lord's message through his prophet:

> *"Look! The virgin will conceive a child!*
> *She will give birth to a son,*

and he will be called Immanuel

(meaning, God is with us)."

When Joseph woke up, he did what the angel of the Lord commanded.

A few days later Mary hurried to the hill country of Judea, to the town where Zechariah lived. She entered the house and greeted Elizabeth. At the sound of Mary's greeting, Elizabeth's child leaped within her, and Elizabeth was filled with the Holy Spirit.

Elizabeth gave a glad cry and exclaimed to Mary, "You are blessed by God above all other women, and your child is blessed. What an honor this is, that the mother of my Lord should visit me! When you came in and greeted me, my baby jumped for joy the instant I heard your voice! You are blessed, because you believed that the Lord would do what he said."

Mary responded,

"Oh, how I praise the Lord.
How I rejoice in God my Savior!
For he took notice of his lowly servant girl,
and now generation after generation will call me blessed.

For he, the Mighty One, is holy,

and he has done great things for me."

Mary stayed with Elizabeth about three months and then went back to her own home.

At that time the Roman emperor, Augustus, decreed that a census should be taken throughout the Roman Empire. (This was the first census taken when Quirinius was governor of Syria.) All returned to their own towns to register for this census. And because Joseph was a descendant of King David, he had to go to Bethlehem in Judea, David's ancient home. He traveled there from the village of Nazareth in Galilee. He took with him Mary, his fiancée, who was obviously pregnant by this time.

And while they were there, the time came for

her baby to be born. She gave birth to her first child, a son. She wrapped him snugly in strips of cloth and laid him in a manger, because there was no room for them in the village inn.

That night some shepherds were in the fields outside the village, guarding their flocks of sheep. Suddenly, an angel of the Lord appeared among them, and the radiance of the Lord's glory surrounded them. They were terribly frightened, but the angel reassured them. "Don't be afraid!" he said. "I bring you good news of great joy for everyone! The Savior—yes, the Messiah, the Lord—has been born tonight in Bethlehem, the city of David! And this is how you will recognize him: You will find a baby lying in a manger, wrapped snugly in strips of cloth!"

Suddenly, the angel was joined by a vast host of others—the armies of heaven—praising God:

> *"Glory to God in the highest heaven,*
> *and peace on earth to all whom God favors."*

When the angels had returned to heaven, the shepherds said to each other, "Come on, let's go to Bethlehem! Let's see this wonderful thing that has happened, which the Lord has told us about."

They ran to the village and found Mary and Joseph. And there was the baby, lying in the manger. Then the shepherds told everyone what had happened and what the angel had said to them about this child. All who heard the shepherds' story were astonished, but Mary quietly treasured these things in her heart and thought about them often. The shepherds went back to their fields and flocks, glorifying and praising God for what the angels had told them, and because they had seen the child, just as the angel had said.

About that time some wise men from eastern lands arrived in Jerusalem, asking, "Where is the newborn king of the Jews?

We have seen his star as it arose, and we have come to worship him."

Herod was deeply disturbed by their question, as was all of Jerusalem. He called a meeting of the leading priests and teachers of religious law. "Where did the prophets say the Messiah would be born?" he asked them.

"In Bethlehem," they said, "for this is what the prophet wrote:

'O Bethlehem of Judah,

you are not just a lowly village in Judah,

for a ruler will come from you

who will be the shepherd for my people

Israel.'"

Then Herod sent a private message to the wise men, asking them to come see him. At this meeting he learned the exact time when they first saw the star. Then he told them,

"Go to Bethlehem and search carefully for the child. And when you find him, come back and tell me so that I can go and worship him, too!"

After this interview the wise men went their way. Once again the star appeared to them, guiding them to Bethlehem. It went ahead of them and stopped over the place where the child was. When they saw the star, they were filled with joy! They entered the house where the child and his mother, Mary, were, and they fell down before him and worshiped him. Then they opened their treasure chests and gave him gifts of gold, frankincense, and myrrh. But when it was time to leave, they went home another way, because God had warned them in a dream not to return to Herod.

About the Author

Francine Rivers has been writing for over twenty years. From 1976 to 1985 she had a successful writing career in the secular market and won numerous awards. After becoming a born-again Christian in 1986, Francine wrote *Redeeming Love* as her statement of faith. Published by Bantam, the book was voted the favorite novel of 1991 by *Affaire de Coeur* readers and was a finalist for the Romance Writers of America (RWA) Choice Award.

Since then, Francine has written The Mark of the Lion trilogy, which consists of *A Voice in the Wind* (a Campus Life Book of the Year winner), *An Echo in the Darkness* (a 1995 ECPA Gold Medallion finalist and recipient of the RWA Rita Award), and *As Sure As the Dawn* (also an

RWA Rita winner.) *The Scarlet Thread* followed, earning Francine a third Rita and qualifying her for the RWA Hall of Fame in July 1997. She was the sixth woman writer in America to receive this honor. *The Atonement Child* was released in 1997 and remained #1 on the CBA best-seller list for four months. Also released in 1997 is what Francine calls her "redeemed" version of *Redeeming Love,* published by Multnomah for the CBA readership. It has remained in the top ten of the CBA best-seller list since its release. *The Last Sin Eater* was released in 1998.

Francine says she uses her writing to draw closer to the Lord, that through her work she might worship and praise Jesus for all he has done and is doing in her life.

She lives in northern California with her husband, Rick. They have three grown children and one grandson.